GROWN UP GAMES

GANGED HOUSE PARTY

TENA SELDAN

plicit Press

CHAPTER 1

AS FAR AS ROOMIES WENT, Tasha and Stacy were as unlikely a pair as possible. Which is exactly why they worked. It helped that they were best friends, too, but the carefree bartender slash dog walker slash model slash whatever paid for shoes, Tasha, was the polar opposite of shy, almost fragile computer programmer, Stacy.

They had been friends since high school, and it was actually Stacy who moved into Tasha's midtown apartment, a gift from her folks while she *'found herself,'* and so it seemed, for the moment at least, that their bond was one that would not be severed by time, or Stacy's climb up the ladder of success that was, apparently, a big part of being an adult.

"How do they look?" Tasha asked, cupping her *Gifts from God,* Stacy's pet name for her breasts, in her hands and lifting them ever so slightly as if they needed the support.

"Your breasts look great," Stacy said, thinking of her shameful cup size, barely a handful!

Tasha had the kind of careless beauty that literally took your breath away. Her slight tan was artificial, yes, but it was so perfectly complimented by every part of her that she really looked like she was born like this. According to her, she was.

Her hair, a high, loose roll on the crown of her head, would look secretarial on Stacy. It looked perfect on Tasha as she finished with her unnecessary but YouTube tutorial perfect make-up, the last of her 'things to do' before she ran out the door, already late for her shift at *Charley's!*

"Who is *Charley*, anyway?" Tasha asked Greg, her manager, quickly, before he gave her his usual 'you're late' speech.

"Charley is the dude you won't work for anymore if you keep doing this!" Greg was strict, at least his voice was. The smile threatening the corners of his mouth betrayed him, though.

"I know," she said, swinging into the bar, putting on her apron, shoving her purse under the counter, and serving her first drink, all at once, it seemed. She was really very good at her job, and the customers liked her, so she knew she would have to mess up monumentally to get herself fired for real.

Charley's had a very specific clientele. It was not the trendy click or the bohemian hippies. No, Charley's was the preferred dive of every laborer and his dog. The place reeked of sweat and manual labor, and the patrons always looked like they'd come straight from the job site to the bar, for a much deserved cold one. Tasha enjoyed them, for the most part, the other part wondering how she was going to find herself serving drinks for minimum wage!

"*Save me, Please!*" She was almost pleading to Stacy as she pushed the metal door at the back of the bar open and lit a cigarette at the same time. She really had a wonderful way of grouping multiple tasks into one effortless stream.

"You tired of being the object of *Jack's* affection,

already?" They called every Charley's customer *Jack*, for no reason in particular.

Jack's fine tonight, on his best behavior actually. I'm just bored, and we know how I get when I'm bored. So really, *save me!"*

Stacy knew, of course, what her friend meant.

On slow nights at Charley's, the customers or Greg would buy her drinks. A lot of drinks. And drunk Tasha plus bored Tasha usually turned into *sneaking out of a stranger's house at 3 AM Tasha*.

"Slow night, then, I take it?" Stacy asked.

"I'm on my third drink," Tasha said, glad to have someone who understood her. Stacy moving in with her really saved her from herself. And it helped that her parents liked Stacy, secretly hoping that some of her ambition would rub off on their princess.

"I'll be right there!"

———

Stacy walked into Charley's about an hour later, to find Tasha and Greg sitting on the wrong side of the bar, listening to one of the *Jacks* telling, very loudly, a story of great consequence. She got the tail end of the conversation as she came up behind her best friend and kissed the side of her face.

"You came," Tasha said, too loud, pulling her savior in for a real hug. Stacy raised her hand to greet Greg and every *Jack* who looked like they were a part of this little group.

"Dead tonight?" she said to Greg, looking around.

"Wednesdays are not our best," Greg said, walking around to the right side of the bar, asking Stacy with his eyes what she'd like to drink.

"Make it interesting," she said, turning to her friend, whom she knew could handle her liquor and just used it as an excuse for promiscuity!

They chatted easily for the rest of the evening, pockets of *Jacks* coming in, having a few, and then leaving. For the most part, the bar's furniture was accessorized by Greg and Tasha, Stacy, and three *Jacks*, the teller of tales called Len, if the name embroidered into the lapel of his coveralls was to be believed. Wednesdays were really the worst days at Charley's, by comparison. This comparison was, of course, made against the dollars in the tip jar on every other good night!

"I need a favor," Stacy said to Greg as she helped him clean up, which was basically turning the chairs over onto the tables. A suddenly sober Tasha was busy at the cash register.

"Sure, what's up?"

"I need Tasha to *not* work on Friday?!" Her familiarity with Greg made it okay to ask him, but his position in the bar's hierarchy meant that she had to *ask* him.

"Fridays are busy, what's this for? It isn't her birthday?"

"No... I've got a work thing and I kinda need a date!"

"As opposed to a regular date?" Greg was pointing to himself!

"She just has a way of getting away that I'm going to need on Friday..."

"So you're looking for a getaway driver," Greg chuckled at his own joke, again pointing to himself.

"Please?"

"I'll make you a deal. If you promise to bring your colleagues in here at least two nights this month, you've got a deal!"

"Deal!"

CHAPTER 2

"DO YOU HAVE A PICTURE OF *TREY*?" Tasha was scrambling for a way to get out of this, thinking of the tips she'd be missing out on Friday.

"No," was the reply, before Stacy realized that she would have to do much better than that if she was going to convince her best friend to serve as her *potential boyfriend's* buffer.

"No fair asking Greg behind my back... Although, I am proud. We'll make a liar of you yet!"

"It was *manipulator* yesterday," Stacy responded, not sure she would ever forgo her goody goody image to become *Tasha*!

"Liar, Manipulator, Potato, Tomatoes..." Tasha tried, always, to sound clever.

"You have no idea what the saying actually is, do you?"

"Nope, and I don't care. I'm still not going!"

The promise of board games and booze wasn't incentive enough for Tasha, who would really rather spend the night plying construction workers with drinks that converted, as the night wore on, to increasingly careless tips. She did live mostly on her parents' dime, but there were still some things she couldn't charge to the credit card they still got the statements for.

"Come on. How many times have I saved you from, well, *you*, and not asked for anything in return?"

" Emotional blackmail? Wow, you are a quick study!"

"I learned from the best," Stacy said, hoping flattery would produce the desired effect.

It did!

Stacy gave Tasha the 4-1-1 on who would be there, and also gave her as much information about Trey as she could fit into the fifteen minutes before she had to leave for work. Tasha was tasked with getting her an outfit, and one for herself, of course, a natural extension of the bribe. Tasha decided, that since she had Stacy's credit card, she'd get her nails and hair done too. There really was no point in arriving at the Royal Geekdom of Fun and Games looking like *a geek*.

Her pampering took her all day, and by the time she and Stacy met in the foyer of their apartment building, she was armed with two outfits, both of which she liked so she would let Stacy 'choose,' and her hair and nails looking like she was the Face of Something.

"You look *nice*," Stacy said, not envious, but letting her know that she knew who had paid for this mini-makeover.

"I always look nice, and you will too when I'm done with you. And before you say anything, I'm going to go light on the make-up, but make-up you will wear!"

Stacy didn't mind, this time. She really did like Trey, and given that this was the first time she'd been asked to his house for games night, she had to make a good impression. Her Plain Jane office look was okay as she programmed computers at work, ogling Trey from a distance. But now he had noticed her, and she needed to do everything to make sure he looked nowhere else.

"You'll like the others," Stacy said as she tried on the first outfit, a grey mini-dress that was suggestive enough to let Trey know she was *open to it,* but sophisticated enough to let her play hard to get!

"Don't sell me on the nerds, honey. I'm really just doing this for you!"

They spent the rest of the evening playing with different make-up looks for Stacy. The Chinese and wine they had for dinner was the only interruption to their make-up trials, that and the constant beeps on Tasha's phone. She had left many a man wanting *more*, in the last month alone.

By the time they went to bed, Tasha was already contemplating responding to one of the messages. She had an insatiable appetite and no shortage of men willing to feed her. She decided, though, that tonight it would be her and her *Ladybug*, and as she slipped into bed post-shower, she pulled her trusted *helper* from her side drawer. It really was her *friend indeed*!

Her room was dark, just how she liked it, and she definitely needed no light for what she was about to do. She started up the *not large enough to be uncomfortable* device, and as it warmed itself up with an almost inaudible hum, she pressed two fingers against herself, to ensure that she was moist and ready.

It didn't take too long.

The tentacles on her Ladybug were firm and soft at the same time, and they sent short, sharp pulses over the outside of her feminine void. Her lips smiled, and she pressed the shaft of the device gently into herself, slipping it easily into her almost too moist canal. She let it sit inside her for a minute, enjoying the lashing she was getting from the pulsating tentacles. After a short while, Tasha moved the instrument in and out of her in measured strokes, with absolutely no need to rush.

Her legs were crossed and uncrossed. Her entire body succumbed to this delicious assault on herself, and she started to shudder, wishing to herself that it was attached to a man. It wasn't, though, and it really was too late for any late-night booty call to be called that, so she just relaxed into her self-manipulation.

As her self-imposed orgasm rippled over her, she found herself thinking about tomorrow. There was no getting out of it now, so she would have to just make the best of it. Although just what making the best of it meant, she had no idea!

CHAPTER 3

THEY ARRIVED at Trey's apartment shortly after 7:30. Stacy looked stunning, Tasha equally so. Tasha wore a strapless mini-dress, mauve with fringe detail. Together they looked like they were on their way to a cocktail party, and not a games evening with a few *overenthusiastic book-worms*. Tasha's words.

"Hello hello, welcome..." Trey said as he opened the door. The shorts and Avengers t-shirt he was wearing made both girls feel like they'd perhaps overdressed.

"This is Tasha," Stacy said, calling on her friend to save her from the embarrassment of having done too much.

"Hello Trey," Tasha said before adding, "we're gonna need to be out of here by midnight. I managed to score us a couple of VIP passes into *Pulse!*"

Trey looked at Stacy, surprised, saying with just his eyes behind trendy frameless spectacles, that he hadn't pegged her for a clubber.

"Come in, please," he said when he finally composed himself.

Stacy and Tasha passed a look between them, Stacy's saying *'thank you,'* and Tasha's saying *'goddamn, he's nice!'*

Trey's apartment wasn't small, even though it had just one bedroom. The living area was divided into lounge, dining room, and kitchen, the spaces identified by furniture and function. The only bathroom was an ensuite off Trey's bedroom. The proportions of it were generous, though.

It was simple, but as far as bachelor pads went, not too bad.

Tasha walked in last, and she was introduced to Tristan, Ethan, and Dale, not formally, but more an *"everyone says hello to Tasha"* as they went about finishing setting up. It wasn't as formal as Tasha had thought it would be. Trey poured them drinks and threw a beer to Dale who was busy setting up Dungeons and Dragons on the dining table. Ethan and Tristan, beers in hand, were staring at popcorn popping in the microwave, literally.

Stacy was right. They weren't half bad-looking. Trey was the best looking, although not typical. He just had a mysterious air about him, like he would walk into a phone booth and exit as *Superman*. Tristan was also not typically handsome, but his size made him attractive. He stood an imposing six-feet eight inches, Tasha thought, and he wasn't skinny. He wasn't fat by regular standards but he was large.

Ethan was tall and lanky, the skinniest of the bunch. Tasha thought immediately of an article she once read and found herself imagining what all their penises looked like. She needed to make this as fun for herself as possible, and this mental game was as good a place as any to start. Dale was obviously handsome, a redhead, with freckles, but there was no denying his good looks. Tasha had always thought the best way to judge looks was by how well your flaws played together. And, in her book, red hair and freckles were definitely flaws!

They were friendly enough, but not nearly as enthusiastic as Tasha had anticipated. She was almost offended, saved by the attention she and Stacy were getting from the host, and that occasionally she would catch one or all three of the others checking her out. She found refuge in drink, but when they sat down to play Dungeons and Dragons, she once again felt like the oddball.

"So what is it that you do," Dale asked halfway through his round. Tristan got up to get drinks but didn't take his eyes off Tasha. She wasn't sure if he knew he was staring. Although, she had just been asked a question that none of them except for Stacy knew the answer to, and so he was probably just being politely attentive, trying to seem interested in her response.

"I'm a bartender," she said, catching herself staring at Tristan as he adjusted something in his own shorts. They were all wearing shorts, just long enough to hide what she thought were probably impressive packages. Tasha almost shook the thought from her head, not sure why she was suddenly so obsessed with seeing these men naked.

"Favorite drink?" Tristan asked as he handed her a glass of store-bought premixed Pina Colada. It wasn't half bad. Again his hand was on his crotch, and again Tasha's eyes followed the up down side to side of his massive fingers. She looked down at his feet too, and then quickly up to his face again.

"Anything with a percentage, really," she responded. They all laughed.

"My kinda woman," said Tristan, bringing his glass to hers.

"You're very big," she said, stating the obvious, bringing the entire room to life with collective laughter once more.

"Yeah, he is quite large," said Dale, obviously looking at Tristan downstairs, who put a hand to cover himself, before mock-punching Dale.

"How do you know?" he asked.

"Oh, I know..." Dale said, winking, a knowing grin on his face.

Ethan, who'd been suspiciously quiet up until now, suddenly asked, "so what do you do for fun?"

Tasha looked at everybody at the table, all eyes again on her. She knew that there was a right answer and a wrong answer, what with everyone at the table having an incredibly analytical mind. She also knew there was a truthful answer, so she decided that she would go with the truth. After all, what were the chances that she would ever see any of them again?

"I have random sex with strangers!"

They all paused, taking in the honesty. "I think we'll be over there playing Snakes and Ladders," Trey said, lifting Stacy from her seat and guiding her to a loveseat in the far corner, a small coffee table with the game already set up.

"Sissy," Tristan said to Trey, before returning his stare to Tasha.

Tasha took a final sip, emptying her Pina Colada down her throat. Then she looked at the three men in front of her, took a sultry breath, and said, in an almost whisper, "and if I'm not wrong, you're all still relative strangers..."

CHAPTER 4

ETHAN STOOD UP ALMOST IMMEDIATELY. He ran his fingers over the top of his shorts, and then pulled them away from himself, looking down into his pants before throwing a 'dare me' look to the men. Tristan laughed loudly and watched Dale stand up and do the same thing. Then he looked at Tasha, wanting to get a reading on her. She just stared calmly at the men threatening to expose themselves.

She looked like she'd seen this behavior a thousand times before. She was a bartender at a pub, he remembered, so she probably had.

Tasha fiddled under the table for just a second, not once taking her eyes off the three. Then, slowly, she lifted her panties with her index finger, held them over the board game, and then let them drop into the table. Her eyes moved down to the crotches of the two standing men. Something moved in Ethan's, Dale putting his hand down his shorts, in an attempt to hide his own arousal. Tristan shifted in his seat, making adjustments to his own crotch now, a growing problem becoming more than a bit obvious.

"Oh to hell with this," Tasha said, standing up. She went

around to Ethan and Dale, and in her usual ninja fashion, she pulled both their shorts down to their knees. Ethan's hand went quickly on himself where Dale's hands already were. Tristan looked over to Trey and Stacy, who had abandoned the game temporarily in favor of acquainting their mouths with each other.

"This night just got a whole lot more interesting," Tristan said, as Tasha walked over to the lounge area, and planted herself on the three division daybed.

She was on her knees, and then put her hand underneath her dress. She ran her fingers over herself, and then very slowly *pretended* to dig into herself. Then she took this finger and put it into her mouth.

"Quick, name the movie," she whispered. But none of them could speak. Ethan and Dale made their way slowly to where Tristan was already half lying on the sofa opposite. He seemed to have no intention to participate, choosing instead the no-pressure position of passive observer!

Nobody answered her. Trey shouted suddenly, "Basic Instinct!"

"Never seen it," Tasha said, ending Trey's involvement in what was about to play out.

She lifted her dress slowly, exposing just enough of the pink perfection between her thighs to let Ethan and Dale know that it was anybody's move now. The two looked at each other, and then back at Tristan, who just shrugged, obviously still a little unsure about what was actually going on here. The massive bulge in his shorts gave away what he hoped this was, though.

Dale finally removed his hands, revealing a rather fat uncircumcised mass. He was fully at attention, still though his foreskin covered his massive head. It would be a pretty penis if it wasn't for the untidiness of his foreskin, Tasha thought. This was in no way a dealbreaker for her, of course, but there really just was a lot of it.

Tasha summoned him to her with her eyes, feeling that he should be rewarded, if for nothing else, for his bravery. She took the thickness between her fingers, and gently tried to push the foreskin back. It soon became obvious that it was not going to go anywhere.

She let the skin rub against her lips, which made him harder. Then she opened her mouth and started to ease him slowly into the back of her throat. He fitted completely, stretching her mouth to capacity in every direction. Then she slowly pushed him from her mouth until just his foreskin was left between her teeth.

"Please, bite..." he asked, almost too politely. She started to bite gently, to which he said, "harder... Please!" So she did, and he went crazy. He held her head so that her mouth stayed on him, as he bent down and put his hands between her thighs, finding her incredibly wet! He didn't pretend, sending a thick middle finger all the way up inside her. Dale couldn't breathe.

They stayed connected this way for a while before Ethan came up, stood next to Dale, and let her see him for the first time. She had guessed correctly. He was long and thick, with what she could only describe as bull's balls, hanging heavy under his long curve. If Dale's penis passed the almost pretty test, Ethan's looked incredibly menacing. She was excited to see how he would maneuver it inside her if they got that far.

By now, though, she knew that they would.

Dale pulled himself from her mouth and removed her dress quickly, scared that she might change her mind. He knelt down in front of her, sucking hard on her nipples in tandem. Ethan took the gap, filling her mouth with his curve. This was definitely the over-enthusiasm she had earlier anticipated.

He slid himself into her mouth as far as he would go, parked for a minute, and then pulled himself completely out. He did this a number of times before hitting the back of her throat with his head in a seamless succession of short thrusts. Tasha had a gag reflex second to none, he thought.

Dale pushed her back on the couch so that he could access her fruit with his mouth, Ethan's height allowing him to stay in her mouth. He nibbled on the delicateness for a while, until his mouth dripped with the sweet nectar flowing from her. Again, he did this for just a minute before bringing himself up and slightly on the couch, positioning his manhood with her femininity. He could wait no longer, evicting Ethan from her mouth as he lay himself on top of her and slid into her in one motion.

"Oh my..." he said as he started to thrust, slowly at first, and then not so slowly. Tasha was tight, but Dale was determined. He got his fatness all the way inside her, thrusting harder. Then he stopped, took a breath, and thrust a little slower, until the excitement overwhelmed him again, at which point he went *ape* again.

Dale stayed inside her as long as he could, brought himself almost to a premature climax, and then pulled himself out of her quickly. He threw Ethan a "you need to get in on this

' look, at which point they swopped positions and Ethan was now positioning Tasha for his comfort as much as hers.

CHAPTER 5

TASHA, on her back further on the daybed, had her eyes on Tristan now. He was standing up, contemplating, it seemed, the removal of his own shorts with the utmost care. She watched him disappear behind the couch and heard the door to the bedroom open and then close. Then music filled the space, the volume rising slowly so that she could still hear Stacy and Trey making out just a little ways away.

Tristan threw a tube at Ethan, and then knelt on the couch, lifting Tasha's head so that he could run his erection across her face. She felt cool between her thighs suddenly as Ethan filled her with too much lube, inserting one, two, and then three fingers into her. He moved these fingers deeper, long thin intruders attempting to stretch her as far as she would go.

Then he fingered her with just one, steadily, determined it seemed to bring her to climax. He was obviously trying to get her as wet as possible. Thankfully, it was working, because she needed it after Dale's too-quick entry, and also because Tristan suddenly pulled his own penis out, revealing in all its magnificence the source of his earlier apprehension.

She knew it wouldn't fit in her mouth, so she started to lick it, hard up against one side and then as hard down the other. Then she worked on his head with her tongue and lips, getting just the top of the huge dome into her mouth. She knew that, at a stretch, she would be able to possibly get at least some of him into her tiny mouth, but not in a way that would be comfortable for either of them.

She worked her mouth down over his perfect ovals. They really were ridiculously perfect, in shape and appearance. And the fact that he was perfectly manscaped only added to this perfection. She had no trouble getting both of them into her mouth, not quite sucking, not quite licking, not quite biting.

"How are you doing that?" Tristan asked, not wanting her to stop. She had found his weak spot.

She couldn't answer, her mouth full. Also, Ethan had once again planted three fingers inside her and she needed to focus. The fact that Dale was licking her toes offered little distraction. It felt incredible, but to distract her it did not.

Ethan pulled his fingers from her eventually, turning her onto her stomach. His slippery hands parted her buttcheeks, exposing the most beautiful *rosebud* he had ever seen. He settled his face between her cheeks and went to work on her with his tongue. She arched her back and raised her beautiful bottom into Ethan's face even more. He loved this, flicking his tongue over the exterior until he could no longer resist the urge to go in. Tristan in the meantime had positioned himself underneath her so that she had ease of access to the parts on him she wanted while giving

Ethan unencumbered access to the parts of her he was enjoying.

Dale licked and sucked her toes a little longer before getting up and going to get drinks.

Ethan pulled her so that she was now on her knees. He dropped the lube directly onto her perfect bubble, rubbing it in, finding her center, and then easing the lube in with just the tip of his finger. He threw the tube onto the rug, working with the excessive lube he had already poured onto her booty.

He slid it from side to side, and then up and down like he was painting a *Picasso*. Then again he found her center with just the tip of his finger, working more and more of the lube into her deliciously tight space. Then he gently eased the length of his finger inside her, pulling her back onto it as he did.

Ethan had really mastered the art of fingering, sending one finger into her front as he settled his thumb in her rear. Parking his thumb in place, he added a second finger to her front and proceeded to conduct a symphony on both crevices. It felt incredible, and her responses to this must have been equally impressive because when she opened her eyes Tristan's own eyes were fixed on her as he ran his own fingers up and down his incredible length.

When Ethan's fingers slipped from her, she became anxious. She wanted to scream *don't go,* but before she could, he had lifted and lowered her onto himself, and was masterfully maneuvering his lengthy curve into her equally tight but exceptionally wet womanhood. It went in easily, but he held her tightly, easing her down on himself, enjoying this process immensely, it seemed.

He got half of himself inside her, paused briefly, and then

lifted her completely off. Then he repeated the exercise, a number of times, before pushing her down on all fours and swiftly driving just half of himself in and out of her, all the while fingering her beautiful behind. She tried to reach for Tristan, but couldn't focus. So Tristan brought himself to her and let her do with his shaft what she wanted, what she could.

She was again licking it, swallowing his perfect sack, doing *her thing* on it before she resumed licking his length. Then she played with his tip with just her tongue, another thing he enjoyed and so she did it for the longest time. Ethan was sending just that much more of his bend into her now, and again she felt she needed to concentrate. After a minute though she surrendered, trusting that he knew what he was doing because quite frankly, he did!

"I wanna nut so bad," Ethan said out loud, ceasing all motion. Tasha wanted to tell him that it was okay, but before she could he was pulling himself out of her. He got up and took the drink from Dale, who looked like he wanted to come back, but knowing that Tristan hadn't had a go yet.

By the look on Tasha's face, she really wanted Tristan to at least try!

CHAPTER 6

JUST THEN A CELLPHONE started ringing somewhere, and everyone looked at Tristan, who, slightly irritated, got up to go and find it. Dale waited as Ethan took his place on the daybed, moving Tasha's mouth onto himself. He waited until Tristan answered his phone, and then he was on her.

Still lying on her stomach, Dale got on top of her and found her tightness, parting her legs a little to allow himself full access. He filled her even quicker this time, much to his apparent relief, and he was thrusting eagerly almost immediately, his eyes on Tristan, who seemed to be caught up in an intense conversation.

His hands on her hips, pressing her into the couch, he went deeper, harder. Tasha's *everything* excited him, and he drove himself into her completely before he realized that he was being more than a little selfish. He was enjoying himself so much that he hadn't thought if Tasha was having a good time.

Dale stopped moving, and whispered in her ear, "is it good?"

She just smiled, raising her booty slightly, allowing him

even better access. He knew that this meant she was good and proceeded to thrust into her with the urgency of a man possessed. He knew that he had just a few minutes before Tristan would be back, and so he needed, desperately, to empty himself.

He moved onto his side, pulling Tasha with him. Lifting her leg, he watched himself move inside her. It was an incredible sight, and Dale could not take his eyes off it. All the way in and all the way out he went, his rock-solid erection making the use of hands unnecessary to guide himself to where he needed to be.

Ethan moved onto his side too, so that her mouth could keep up with its magic on his meat. He saw Tristan finish up on the phone, and wondered who he would move off Tasha. But the friendly giant just got himself a drink and sat back on the couch, watching, waiting.

Dale was incredibly close now, and he closed his eyes. As he shuddered, shaking his juices into Tasha, he moaned, loudly. Tristan started a slow clap, and he wasn't sure if this was sarcasm. Everyone knew how sarcastic Tristan could be.

As he rolled onto his back, exhausted, Dale slipped out of her. The sound of his exit made Tasha chuckle, and almost choke on Ethan, who was holding her head hard, moving her mouth up and down on himself, also incredibly close. Courtesy required that he tell her that he was about to release an incredible amount of thick goo from his curve, but unfortunately for Tasha, he had already worked himself past the point of no return.

Ethan couldn't breathe, so he couldn't speak. And so he had no way of warning her of what was about to happen.

And then it happened!

Tasha took it in her stride, though. She took him deeper

into her mouth so that the tangy liquid projecting out of him went directly down her throat. This was a good move too because there was quite a lot of it.

Ethan didn't move as he pumped an incredible amount of love juice into her mouth and down her throat. She didn't move until she had swallowed every last drop. More perfect it could not be if he had planned it, Ethan thought!

He lifted her mouth off himself and also rolled onto his back. He couldn't take his eyes off of Tasha though, looking at her with curious interest, and also wondering what he could do to please her now. He really felt that she deserved it. He also just felt like he wasn't a man until he had brought her to a real orgasm.

Ethan was thinking too much!

Tasha stood up now and went over to Tristan on the couch. She got down between his thick, long legs, and put her tongue to his scrotum. She licked the orbs gently for a minute before letting them slip, one at a time, into her mouth. She ran her teeth over their smooth surface, occasionally biting just hard enough to make Tristan wince.

"I really want to be inside you..." he grunted.

"I really want you inside me," she said!

His meat was against the side of her face, Tristan hitting it against her cheek as if confirming that he'd be too big for her tiny self. Tasha never shied from a challenge, though, and she really wanted to prove to herself if it was impossible. She knew that it couldn't not be!

Could it?

She lifted herself off the floor, and straddled him, her legs stretched to almost a full split. She rubbed the outside of herself against his monster, half gauging its actual size, and a half because she really needed to feel him against her.

She placed her knees on his thighs, positioning herself

directly over him. She wasn't sure if she trusted the lube that Ethan had plied into her, or the lava still warm inside her that had erupted from Mt. Dale, but she was lowering herself into him, holding herself up by bracing her arms on his neck. She was in full control, and he knew that if this was going to happen, this was how it needed to be.

His head pressed hard against her, slipping away from her entrance. He held it up with one hand and kept it straight so that Tasha could if she wanted, get it inside herself easier. He just held onto his meat and kept it pointing up. This was the extent of his involvement, too scared to move, in case he broke her.

Tasha pressed harder down, and she started to give way. Caught off guard, she lifted herself off him, quickly. As quickly though, she settled back over him, pushing herself down so that his head made entry. Then neither of them moved, Tasha, breathing deep, knowing that timing was everything now!

CHAPTER 7

TASHA HELD HERSELF UP, and started to move slowly in circles on just Tristan's thick tip. Her tightness made this an exercise requiring the utmost precision. She had just surrendered herself to Ethan. There was no way that this surrender was possible now. All Tristan could do to assist was spread his legs a bit, to allow her more space to work. This was just what she needed.

Very slowly, she managed an inch passed his head. She moved on just this inch plus head, in agonizingly slow circles. Then she raised and lowered herself on just this short measurement of the massive man before resuming the slow, sensual circles.

"Are you okay," he asked

"Incredible..." she lied.

"You need to relax. If this is going to happen, then it's going to happen. But you've been awesome, and I really don't *expect* this... You know that right?"

"Of course, I know. But I'm really enjoying myself. Aren't you?" Tasha wasn't moving now, distracted by this conversation that was really bordering on awkward.

"Oh, I am... I am..."

"Then Shhh..." She pushed herself down another inch, and then another. Soon she was up to five inches plus his large head. The more of him that was inside her, the less uncomfortable it was, she noticed. But she also knew that she definitely could not rush it. He was going to get as far inside her as her body would allow, but it would have to be one or two inches at a time.

The good thing was that they both knew this. Tristan also knew and accepted that he would not be able to get every inch of himself into her, no matter how ambitious she was. It was just a physical impossibility.

But what they had managed, together, so far, was incredible. And Tristan really just wanted her to relax now and enjoy what she had managed, already having given him much more than he expected her to give.

Tasha pushed herself up and off him, slowly. Everything about their *union* seemed to be happening in slow motion. It was perfect in its choreography, even though Tristan was feeling more and more like just taking a hold of her waist, and taking the reigns now. He had to keep reminding himself that this was just not possible, for the moment at least. As imposing as he was, *imposition* was the last thing he could do right now.

Ethan lifted her from the back off of Tristan, carrying her back to the daybed. He laid her down on her back and ran his fingers gently over her now-sensitive lips. He watched her with admiration, impressed by the valiance of her efforts. Knowing his friend, though, he knew that Tristan was just too nice a guy to do anything that would cause her discomfort.

He also knew though, that his friend would really like the opportunity to have a full orgasm facilitated by the beautiful female who had so willingly allowed them all to play. And he would do everything he could to make this happen.

With his eyes, he called Tristan over to where he was now teasing Tasha with his tongue. He was moving his tongue over her lips with such precision, placating her body, getting her ready to receive. She thought she was, but everybody knew she wasn't, not for Tristan anyway.

He moved his tongue inside her now, as Tristan reclined next to them on the daybed. He lay on his back, desperate to touch himself, but resisting the urge, knowing from experience that Ethan had a plan. They'd worked as a tag team before, and Tristan knew that his buddy was skilled at providing the needed distraction to allow him to orgasm. So he just put his hands under his head and watched the master at work.

Ethan now sent his tongue into Tasha. It was serpentine, much like him. Long and far-reaching, she firstly wanted him to stop, because she was feeling a little tender. But then what he was doing made sense, and she relaxed into the couch, let her knees fall at her side, and closed her eyes.

She was aware of Tristan but could do nothing for him, the bevy of mini-blasts shooting from inside her already in full swing. Ethan was managing with his tongue what he had mastered with his fingers, and like his fingers, this felt intrusive until it did not.

Ethan seemed to enjoy the fusion of flavors emanating from her. Each time she burst, he lapped it up hungrily, sending his tongue deeper into her *still-tightness*. The eruptions were small, the bursts measured, and Tasha knew that this had nothing to do with her, and everything to do with the skill of the snake between her legs.

When Ethan turned her over, her eyes fell on Dale, who seemed comfortable on the couch that was Tristan's go-to place. He had a drink in hand, and it was he who now seemed to assume the position of a passive observer. His observation was not passive, though, because he was really pulling hard on himself, his *fat little man* glistening in the dim light thanks to the lube.

Ethan brought her up onto all fours, a position she was extremely comfortable with. He parted her cheeks and planted his curve between them, sliding it hard up and down against her rosebud, squeezing her cheeks together as he did.

Suddenly she felt a bit of pressure, and then Ethan was easing his curve into the one place no man had yet gone, no man tonight at least. Her tightness in front was similar to the tightness Ethan was now exploring. His exploration was so deliberate though, so controlled, that again Tasha found it incredibly easy to surrender to him.

He got all the way inside her now, knowing somehow that there was more to have in the rear. The curve of his cock fit perfectly, too, and when he started to thrust, gently, easily thanks to the lube, the ecstasy rippled over her back and made her lose her mind. She looked over at Tristan now, for the first time since his arrival, and even though Ethan was exceptional, she couldn't help but wish that it was Tristan.

CHAPTER 8

ETHAN'S ARMS snaked around her thighs, and he pulled her back until she was literally sitting on him. He moved her up and down on himself, moving her towards Tristan at the same time. He parted his legs, allowing Ethan to work his way between them. He knew what they were about to attempt, and he really hoped it would work. He needed it to work but he also didn't want to get his hopes up.

With himself still inside her, Ethan carefully placed Tasha over Tristan's throbbing tool, Tristan again holding it in place. They were military in their precision, and although Tasha was anxious about the pending invasion from the front, she was relaxed by the almost protection from behind.

Slowly, Tristan started to disappear inside her. He watched as inch after inch vanished. Tasha couldn't look, keeping her eyes on Tristan's face. Five inches and then six disappeared, and then Ethan pushed himself, and her, forward a bit. Seven inches were gone now, and they almost made it to eight but then Tasha whimpered, and they all knew that maximum entry had been reached.

Ethan eased her forward a bit more so that Tasha's hands now rested on Tristan's chest. He stroked the inside of her booty, gently, moving her forward and then back with each stroke. This moved her up and down on the massive accomplishment that was almost eight inches inside her now. Tristan was ecstatic, and it showed on his face.

"There we go... There we go..." Ethan said.

"You're not too uncomfortable?" Tristan asked.

Tasha couldn't answer, planting her fingers into Tristan's chest, holding herself off the rest of Tristan, but thoroughly enjoying the parts of him inside her. She didn't even think of Ethan. She didn't need to. He just knew exactly what was what, and he was helping, not unintentionally Tasha knew, to ensure that no more than the *almost eight* got into her.

Tristan held her hips but made no attempt to move her. He was caught up in the completeness of his own pleasure, trying at the same time to focus on Tasha's comfort and pleasure. He tried to meet Ethan's eyes with his, to say thank you. But Ethan's eyes were closed, him caught up in his own revery.

Ethan came close and paused. Came incredibly close again, and stopped completely. When he came close again, he had to pull out completely, needing a break, not wanting to go over just yet. He went over to Dale and replaced him on the couch, Dale taking up the position that Ethan just had.

He struggled to make entry initially, the thickness a hindrance in this new territory. Also, he needed to ensure that he didn't disturb the *Tristan Tasha Union*. He knew he would not be forgiven if he in any way upset the rhythm they had just established.

He pushed his hand into the small of her back, sliding

her just a bit up Tristan's shaft. Then he guided himself into her again, needing to get inside her despite the recent orgasm he'd just had at his own hands on the couch.

Suddenly it gave, and he was in. Dale was the most enthusiastic of the three, no doubt, and his enthusiasm hadn't waned despite the multiple orgasms he had had already. His thrusting was vigorous, moving Tasha as vigorously up and down on Tristan. It took them a minute, but then they accepted this new pace, but when almost nine inches of him were now inside Tasha, she knew that she would need to assume some control.

"Wait... Wait..." she said.

Despite himself, Dale stopped moving, which stopped the movement over Tristan, who was not moving at all.

Tasha took a deep breath and then started to move her waist in small circles. She had to start small, the thickness in both her holes incredible. She took another breath and made her circles just a little bigger. Dale didn't move too now, enjoying the push and pull of this new *thing* Tasha decided to do.

Tristan shook his head in disbelief. His hands went to her waist and then off. Then again he was holding her waist, needing to touch her, but not wanting to interrupt her. He reached for her neck and held her head so that their eyes met, completing their connection. Dale reached around her and squeezed her nipples hard before squeezing her entire breasts, as hard.

Tasha, eyes locked with the man she was determined to bring to orgasm, made her circles that much bigger, and when Tristan had what was essentially his first orgasm, he let out a loud, guttural, *hallelujah*, and brought himself up so that he could kiss Tasha on her mouth.

Dale finished up and left the two, still connected, to enjoy the aftermath of this battle they had both won!

CHAPTER 9

THERE WAS *nothing boring about this night, thankfully*, Tasha thought. And there was certainly nothing boring about the three very different men now standing over her, the wheels of lust spinning in their heads, obviously trying to think of how best to bring this night to an epic end. Tasha could almost see these thoughts, through their eyes. It looked like they were trying to solve a very complicated algorithm.

Her eyes went to the love seat that Stacy and Trey had occupied just moments earlier. It was empty, the bedroom door to the left of it closed. *Well done, Stacy*, Tasha thought, before returning her attention to the challenge before her, a challenge that she felt more than up to, she being the one who successfully conquered each of them, really.

She sized them up, contemplating her own closing strategy. That they fitted was not the question. Where each of them would go, at once, was what she was trying to decide. Tasha's own thought process must have been obvious, to Tristan, at least. He walked over to the table and filled four glasses with just enough rum to allow each of them the necessary pause to figure their next move out.

When he handed them each a glass, Tasha looked at him in the half-light of the room and wondered what the relationship was between him and Trey. They did, she realized in her lust-filled haze, look remarkably similar, Tristan the heavier of the two though, obviously. She remembered what he had just done to her as she sipped the strong dark liquid slowly. He really was a beast, and she wondered, to her surprise, how agile he was, for his weight.

Tasha liked heavy men, she really did. She enjoyed feeling a man, and not having to look for him. So, as she took another sip, she made up her mind who would be on top, of her at least. Just the thought of him, moving all of himself on her and in her, made her shiver deep inside. The telltale drip down her thighs as her gaze fixed on Tristan made him smile.

He too was watching her closely.

What to do with Ethan and Dale was really a lingering thought in the back of her mind now. The real prize, she knew, for all of them, lay nestled not so snuggly between her legs, open wide now as she reclined on the sofa, sipping the last of the rum and letting it linger in her mouth. She really loved the taste of rum.

Tristan emptied his glass into his mouth and swallowed hard. He got onto the couch, taking one of Tasha's legs in hand, running his tongue from her foot all the way to the glassy liquid still flowing from her. He hovered over her opening, and went instead for the opposite thigh, again with his tongue. Tasha instinctively tried to wrap her legs around his head, her body desperate for him to make contact with *ground zero*. He used his large hands to gently keep her legs where they were, determined to take his time.

Again, he was hovering just above the place she desperately wanted him to touch, and Tasha felt the hot and cold of the air coming from his mouth against her, and again she quivered. She felt like she was going to explode, and she did, a little. This sudden eruption didn't surprise Tristan at all, testament to his experience with what he was doing!

He'd done this before, with many others. Tasha wondered how many others it took for him to master this skill. She arched her back, the top of her head on the couch, her eyes to the door that hid Stacy and Trey, closing them as she sent another squirt directly into Tristan's waiting mouth.

"Are you related?" she asked, suddenly, not sure where the question came from.

"Shhh," Ethan grunted, lowering his large scrotum directly into her mouth. "How about a cuppa tea," he asked, in a terrible English accent.

Tasha ran her tongue over the fine hairs covering the **cannonballs** in her mouth. Her skill caught Ethan off-guard again, sending him and his *macadamias* tumbling backward and landing on the rug. Tasha started to laugh, silenced almost immediately by the insertion of Dale's thick member into her mouth.

Dale planted his knees onto the sofa, on either side of Tasha's head, determined not to go the way of his friend. He moved his thickness hard against Tasha's teeth, making her acutely away of the fact, once more, that he was not circumcised. His fingers fumbled over her breasts as he began to take her mouth. He went in deep, pulling out just enough to leave his foreskin between her teeth.

"Bite it," he pleaded, again too polite

She did...

Dale pulled hard on her round mounds, and then took

her taut perfectly pink nipples between his fingers, and pulled harder. She moaned, silently, her mouth incredibly full. Tasha's groin threatened another eruption, her insides yearning to be addressed. But Tristan seemed too content with just bringing her to mini-orgasm after mini-orgasm, each one doing little in the way of providing any sort of relief.

She didn't see that Ethan had recovered, and was standing behind Tristan. He tapped him on his shoulder after a minute, and Tristan gave up his position, rather reluctantly, to his lanky friend, who wasted no time slithering between her legs.

By the time she realized the tap-out situation between her thighs, it was too late. Ethan went in fast and hard. He was so deep inside her that she gasped, her mouth opening just enough for Dale to settle himself sack-deep down her throat. Ethan was obviously exacting revenge for his embarrassing exit from her mouth earlier, repaying her with precision strokes of his long bend.

It wasn't even uncomfortable this time. Tristan had created such a longing down below that she was desperate for anyone in her *not so hard to reach* the place. *Anyone* was Ethan, and she appreciated the aggressiveness of his thrusting, exactly what she needed after Tristan's tantalizing, but almost too gentle, mouthing.

As Dale pulled his foreskin from her mouth, the end of his still rock solid soldier dripping in his own juices, Ethan let out an excited yelp. He hadn't intended it, he hadn't wanted it, his ego needing to punish her a little longer. But just a few seconds after Dale's deposit down her throat, he too was exploding inside her, writhing as his climax came over him in a quick succession of violent waves.

CHAPTER 10

TRISTAN WATCHED as they detangled from each other, leaving Tasha still on her back, still aching. He bit his lip, wondering whether to savor her a little longer. Then, resuming prime position with the fullness of his bulk, he inched his way inside her, watching her face soften in appreciation.

She had been punished enough!

He had hoped that she would take all of him, this time, since she had, in his mind, been sufficiently prepared. He could still feel that a part of him was outside her wetness, and even though he wanted to feel the full depth of her, it really was an exercise requiring the utmost consideration.

Tristan's size, and his *size*, made it quite possible for him to split the lithe Tasha in two, literally!

She wrapped her legs as far around him as they would go. He bent his knees a bit, giving himself both leverage and control. Then he wasn't moving, allowing her to make the needed adjustments underneath his mass. Tasha raised and lowered herself into him, ever so slightly, determined too it seemed to experience all of him.

"Wow," he grunted.

"Wow yourself," she moaned.

"Yip, it's a very big wow," Ethan joked, high-fiving Dale on the couch opposite, who was remembering fondly that he had been the first to experience the tightness of Tasha.

Tristan and Tasha struggled to find a rhythm again. Although, watching them, you wouldn't have thought it. He went in carefully as far as she would allow, and she moaned deliciously every time he got as far as he could. They seemed aware of their audience, playing to them almost.

This was definitely not the case, because the pair waiting for their bodies to sync hadn't even noticed that Stacy and Trey had exited the room, and were now side by side with Ethan and Dale on the couch, taking in the spectacle playing out before them.

"I'm sorry," Tasha whispered, not sure what for.

" Don't be..." Tristan grunted. " You're incredible!"

Again she was trying to receive more of him. She breathed in as she pushed herself up against him, into him, willing more of him into her. But there just didn't seem to be any more space for the man-mountain to maneuver.

Tasha thought of turning them over, so that she straddled him, like before. But then she remembered that he didn't make it all the way in then either, partly because of her anxiety, but mostly because he was too much body for her tiny self. She let her legs fall off of him now, spreading them as far as they would go. Wrapping her arms around his neck, she began to move just her waist, into his in, out to his out.

Her body finally understood what she was trying to achieve. Without warning, the final few inches of Tristan's mammoth member were inside her, and she couldn't breathe. His knees gave with this full access and his weight rested completely on her. He thrust into her, gentle long thrusts, savoring this conquest, and then he lifted himself just enough so that she could get air into herself and her body could go to work.

And work it did!

Tristan had one hand on the top of her head, the other gripped the edge of the daybed. He seemed to be pushing her onto him or pushing himself into her. Actually, the opposite was true and he was trying to measure his excitement and control if not the depth of his invasion, then at least the intensity!

Tasha's face was to his chest, and she managed quite easily to get his nipples, one at a time, into her mouth, which she masterfully worked with the same skill that saw Ethan plummet to the ground. She wrapped her legs around him again, getting a little more hold this time, given that he was now all the way inside her. She tried to move a little, but this was awkward since she was really hanging from the tree that was Tristan.

"Don't move... I got you," he whispered and then proceeded to deliver a series of masterful strokes that sent every part of Tasha's body into a frenzy. She was shaking, she was shuddering. She was cold and then incredibly hot. She was trembling, and then she wasn't. All the while Tristan drove himself all the way inside her, and pulled himself almost all the way out, letting just his head linger in her, guidance for the next delicious stroke.

He moved over her and inside her with a beauty that was almost biblical. The strength of Samson with the gentleness of David. She wasn't religious by any definition but she now found herself thanking the heavens. Their audience also moved closer, sensing it seemed that both their players were close.

It was Tasha who surrendered first. Her climax was silent, but her body was screaming. She really was a silent moaner, and not even the behemoth that was Tristan would change that. Her body was in ecstasy, every cell on her skin's surface alive, and screaming. He looked down at her face, her head thrashing from side to side, her mouth open, the screams visible on her face even though no sound seemed to escape her. Her groin moved in deep circles against him, maximizing the last of this moment, not sure if he too had gone over yet.

He hadn't, and it was time.

Both his hands now gripped the edge of the sofa, his elbows against her shoulders. He really was a Goliath of a man. If before he had been gentle, now he was not. And Tasha would have it no other way. The urgency of his thrusts reignited her own passions, and soon she was headed for another collision, knowing somehow that they would miss each other on this particular highway to heaven. Everything about Tristan let her know that he too was now close.

He filled her completely, his hot wet man-juice dripping out of her almost as quickly as it had found her depths. The fire was ablaze again inside her, even as she knew that he was almost out. But in true gentlemanly fashion, Tristan did not move until she had managed, mostly on her own this time, to use him to get herself over one last time.

They lay there, unable to move for a minute, the room coming into focus slowly.

"Same time again next week," Trey asked, before sweeping Stacy up off the sofa and carrying her to his room again, inspired no doubt by what he had just witnessed!

ABOUT THE AUTHOR

Tena Seldan is an emerging erotica author of many erotica kinks and sub-genres. Be sure to check out other books and leave a review if this story got you hot!

Visit my blog at Tena Seldan Blog

Join my newsletter for exclusive previews

Tena Seldan Newsletter

Sign up for Free Stories from Xplicit Press Authors

Xplicit Press Author Updates

Like Xplicit Press on Facebook

Follow Xplicit Press on Twitter

Readers: I want to expand a few of the stories to see where the characters can be explored further. If there are any of the stories that you would like to read more about again, I'd love to hear from you!

Keep In Touch
Tena Seldan
info@tenaseldan.com